God Must Like Cookies, Too

God Must Like Cookies, Too

by Carol Snyder
Illustrated by Beth Glick

The Jewish Publication Society
Philadelphia–Jerusalem
5753–1993

With special thanks to my editor
Alice Belgray

Text copyright © 1993 by Carol Snyder
Illustrations copyright © 1993 by Beth Glick
Jacket illustration copyright © 1993 by Beth Glick
First edition. All rights reserved.
Manufactured in the United States of America.
Book design by Edith T. Weinberg
The Jewish Publication Society
Philadelphia – Jerusalem

Library of Congress Cataloging-in-Publication Data

Snyder, Carol.
  God must like cookies, too / by Carol Snyder; illustrated by Beth Glick.
— 1st ed.
    p.   cm.
  Summary: A young girl goes to temple with her grandmother, where she enjoys
the Shabbat service and anxiously awaits the promised cookies she will have at the
Oneg Shabbat after the service.
  ISBN 0-8276-0423-8
  [1. Sabbath — Fiction. 2. Jews — Fiction. 3. Grandmothers — Fiction.] I. Glick,
Beth, ill. II. Title.
PZ7.S68517Gn   1993
[E] — dc20   92 – 26886
                                                                              CIP
                                                                              AC

10 9 8 7 6 5 4 3 2 1

To my granddaughter
Cori Michelle
who fills my heart with love

I love to go to temple with Grandma.
When I put on my silky blue dress with the
    lace collar, she doesn't say,
 "It's too fancy."
She just says, "Beautiful."

We walk to Grandma's temple holding hands.
My hand smells perfumy good from her lotion.
Grandma says, "After Shabbat services, there's
    a cookie party called an Oneg Shabbat, to
        give us delight in the Sabbath.
And you can have any three cookies you
    want."
"God must like cookies, too," I say.

I can already taste them — all sugary, maybe
with a dot of jelly or pink icing in the center.
"Yum yum, um um. I sure do love a good
cookie," I say, "almost as much as I love
spending all day with you, Grandma."

At temple, Grandma likes the seats with
    cushions.
I like the slippery chairs.
They're easier for wiggling and sliding.

"Grandma," I whisper into the quiet, "the man next to me had no supper. His belly is rumbling. He's very hungry. He needs a cookie now."

Grandma hugs my head to her side, laughs, then whispers, "I think he had chicken soup and matzoh balls just like you. It's not cookie time yet, dear.

Look around. There are wonderful things to see."

When the rabbi calls Grandma up to the bema
   to read part of a psalm, she takes me with
      her and whispers, "The bema is like a little
         stage. And we read a psalm to set a
            peaceful mood for praying."
We walk together proudly like the queen and
   princess in my new library book.

I watch the Sabbath candles flicker.
The flames dance with joy.

I help with Psalm 84.
First it's Grandma's turn. In a loud voice she
  says,
"As the sparrow finds a home, and the
  swallow has a nest where she rears
    her young,
So do I seek out your altars,
O Lord of Hosts, my Sovereign God."
Then I say the words Grandma whispers
  to me:
"Happy are those who dwell in Your house;
  they will sing Your praise forever."
That sounds like how I feel when I sleep over
  at Grandma's.

When we get back to our seat, I ask,
"Now do I get a cookie?"
"Not yet, darling," Grandma answers. "First
we'll hear music sweeter than a room full
of cookies."

While I wait to hear the music, Grandma reads
    out loud with everyone.
She lets me look at her prayer book.
There are a lot of words in it but no pictures.

I can only read pictures, so I play with
    Grandma's bracelet instead.
Then I play with her earrings.

Then I play with a baby who's hanging over
his mommy's shoulder.

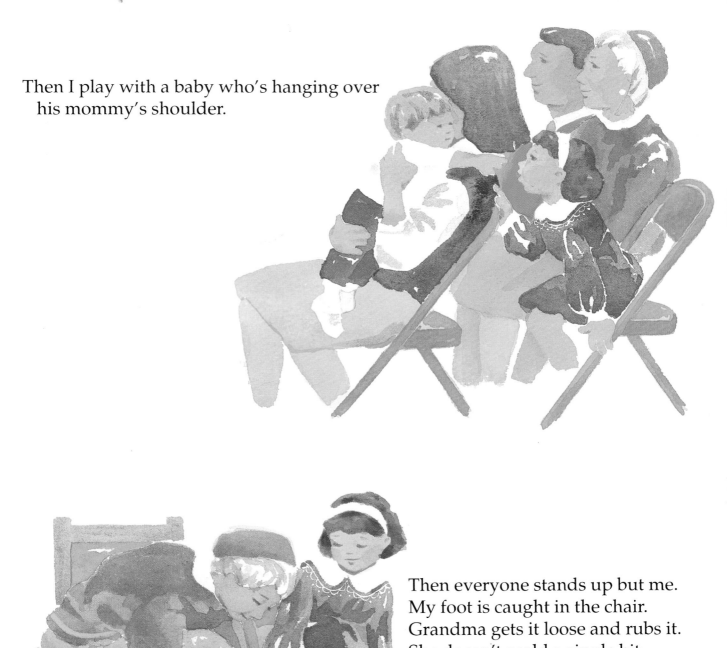

Then everyone stands up but me.
My foot is caught in the chair.
Grandma gets it loose and rubs it.
She doesn't scold a single bit.
I like going to temple with Grandma.

Next, everyone sings, "Shema Yisrael Adonai
    Elohenu Adonai Ehad."
I like the way it sounds. It makes me ice-skate
    in my mind the way Grandma and
        I skated slowly this afternoon at the rink
        at Rockefeller Center.
The singing in temple makes me feel I can do
    anything.
If we skated to temple music, I think we'd
    glide and jump and spin. We'd turn quickly
        and spray ice with the edge of our skates.
I skate my fingers along the back of my chair.
I also like to peek around to see who's looking
    at me.

Then the rabbi talks and talks.
I like to hear the big words, but his voice gets
    far away.
I get sleepy, so I curl up on my chair and lean
    my head on Grandma's lap.
She "nices" my head. Her hands feel so soft on
    my hair.
I remember her hands feeling nice on mine this
        morning at the museum where she teaches
        people to make sculptures out
of clay. We got all mushy and muddy. Then all
    soapy cleaning up. All the students tried to
        make the clay look like my face.

Now I touch the smooth velvet buttons on
  Grandma's sleeve.
So round, like cookies.
And I run my fingers over her pink polished
  fingernails,
So smooth, like the icing on cookies.
And the people sing "Ein Kelohenu."
And the coffee smell sneaks out under the
  folding doors.
I open one eye.

Someone is saying the prayer
     for the wine.
He sips from the kiddush cup.
I look to see if he gets a wine mustache the
     way I got one on Passover,
but I'm too far away to tell.

Then someone slices the challah and says the
     motzi the same way we say it in nursery
     school.
I like challah, but I like cookies better.
My eyes shut.

I think about this afternoon when it was my
turn to take Grandma to my favorite places.
On the carousel in the park we both picked
purple horses that went up and down.

Then I took her to the dog run.
We watched little dogs and big dogs, spotted
   dogs and snow white balls of fur, chase each
   other around in circles.
We chased each other, too.
And laughed so hard we had to sit down and
   rest on a bench.

I wake up when people close their
prayerbooks with a giant clap.
"Now do I get a cookie?" I ask sleepily.

"Yes, sweetheart. Now you get a cookie,"
  Grandma says.
"It's time for the Oneg Shabbat. Now we can
  welcome the Sabbath with joy for the rest
  and happiness it brings everyone."

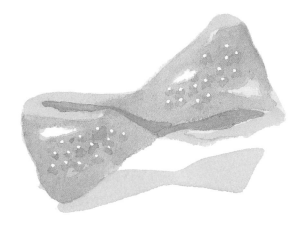

And then I get cookies.
Any three I want. So many to look at.
I wonder which one God would choose.
I choose the round one with jelly, a sugary
    bowtie, and a cookie with chocolate chips.
I also get apple juice and a piece of challah.

And everyone says, "How nice to see you,"
    and "My, how you've grown!"
And Grandma kisses me on the tip of my nose.

I snuggle with Grandma. The cookies are all
gone inside my tummy, but in the dreamy
place inside my mind I'll always picture
Grandma and me sharing favorite things.
I love going to temple with Grandma.
It's sweeter than cookies.

Grandma brings me back to her apartment
    because Mom and Dad are on a trip.
We curl up on her sofa bed. We giggle, and I
    say, "We're big friends, right, Grandma?"
And she says, "Right."
And we go to sleep happy as can be.